vipo Visits the Taj Mahal

Why should you respect others?

Go to **www.av2books.com**, and
enter this book's unique code.

BOOK CODE

D 2 2 4 7 9 8

AV² by Weigl brings you media enhanced
books that support active learning.

First Published by

VipoLand Incorporated
32nd East Street No 3-32,
City of Panama,
Republic of Panama

Published by AV² by Weigl
350 5th Avenue, 59th Floor New York, NY 10118
Website: www.av2books.com

Library of Congress Control Number: 2015946422

ISBN: 978-1-4896-3899-1 (hardcover)
ISBN: 978-1-4896-3900-4 (single user eBook)
ISBN: 978-1-4896-3901-1 (multi-user eBook)

Editor: Katie Gillespie
Project Coordinator: Alexis Roumanis
Art Director: Terry Paulhus

Printed in the United States of America in Brainerd, Minnesota
1 2 3 4 5 6 7 8 9 0 19 18 17 16 15

082015
100715

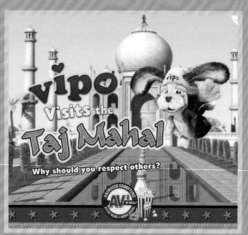

MORAL OF THE STORY

For thousands of years, parents and teachers
have used memorable stories called fables to
teach simple moral lessons to children.

In the Vipo by AV² series, three friends travel
to different countries around the world. They
help people learn many important life lessons.

In *Vipo Visits the Taj Mahal*, Vipo and his friends
teach a snake to respect others. The snake
learns that it is best to consider the feelings of
others and act respectfully toward them.

This AV² media enhanced book comes alive with...

Animated Video
Watch a custom animated movie.

Try This!
Complete activities and hands-on experiments.

Key Words
Study vocabulary, and complete a matching word activity.

Quiz
Test your knowledge.

Vipo Visits the Taj Mahal

Why should you respect others?

AV² Storytime Navigation

KEY WORDS

TRY THIS

Quiz

X CLOSE

PLAY/PAUSE MOVIE

HOME

VIDEO LENGTH

VOLUME

INFO — TITLE INFORMATION

3

The Characters

Vipo
I am a flying dog.
I travel with my friends
to different places. I am
the leader of our group.

The Story

One day, Vipo, Henry, and Betty were flying over Agra, India.

"Is that the Taj Mahal?" asked Betty.

"It's beautiful," said Henry.

"Look," said Vipo. "There's a market over there."

The three friends decided to visit the market.

8

At the market, they found an old man talking to an elephant.
"This performance is very important, Anad," said the old man.
"Hello," said Vipo. "Will you be putting on a show today?"
"Yes," said Anad. "But our last show at the Taj Mahal
didn't go very well."
"What happened?" asked Betty.
"Our snake ruined the act," said the old man.

"You have a snake?" asked Vipo.

"Yes," said Anad. "He's in that vase over there."

Just then, the snake shot out of the vase and hissed.

"Oh no!" cried Betty in fear.

"Don't worry," said the old man. "Mani always does that."

"That's why we didn't do well in our last act," said Anad.

"What did Mani do at your last show?" asked Vipo.

"Mani scared an elephant named Shakira at our last show," said Anad. "Everyone left the show in panic." "If he does it again, we will not be invited back to the Taj Mahal," said the old man.

"I have an idea," said Betty.

Betty bought a flute from a merchant, and started to play. Mani looked stunned, and started to dance around. "You charmed the snake!" cheered the old man. "Quickly, let's make our way to the Taj Mahal. Our show is about to start."

When they arrived at the Taj Mahal, the old man started the show.

First, he walked over a bed of nails.

The audience cheered!

Then, the old man walked across hot coals.

The audience clapped their hands.

"Now, it's time for Mani the snake to dance,"
announced the old man.

Mani poked his head out of his vase.

"I won't come out unless I can scare people," he said.

Just then, Shakira the elephant arrived.

"I know what to do!" exclaimed Vipo.

He blew into Betty's flute and Mani started to dance.

The crowd cheered.

Shakira saw the snake and got scared.

She fell backwards onto the grass.

Anad helped Shakira to her feet.

"It's okay," said Anad. "Mani can't hiss at you while someone is playing the flute."

Shakira watched Mani dance.

"He is harmless, isn't he?" asked Shakira.

"Yes," laughed Anad. "He tries very hard to be tough."

When Vipo stopped playing, Shakira sat down.

"Thank you," said Shakira. "I am no longer afraid of Mani."

"You're welcome," said Vipo. "I'm happy we could help."

Mani looked sad.

"I don't like it when you use the flute to control me," said Mani.

"If you were more respectful of others, we would not have to play music to control you," said Vipo.

"I don't like feeling scared," added Shakira.

Mani felt bad.

"In the future, I won't scare others," promised Mani.

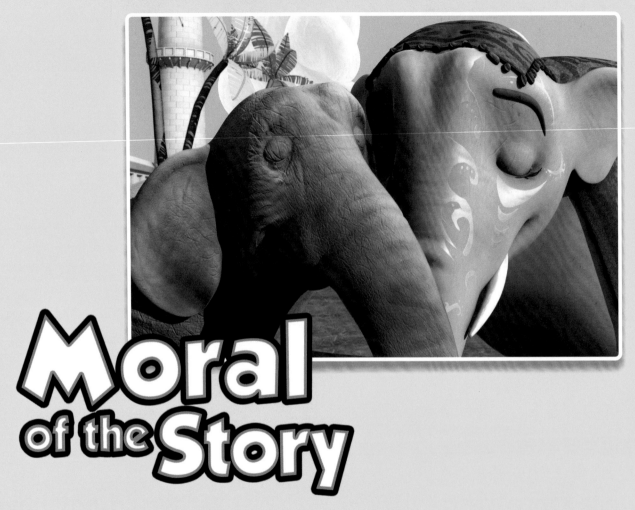

Moral of the Story

It is best to respect others.
If you consider the feelings of others,
they will be nicer to you in return.

vipo Visits the Quiz
Taj Mahal

1
Where did Vipo, Henry, and Betty meet Anad?

2
Where does Mani live?

3
What does Mani like to do to others?

4
How did Betty charm Mani?

5
What did the old man walk on?

6
Who made Mani dance at the show?

Check out www.av2books.com for your animated storytime media enhanced book!

1 Go to www.av2books.com

2 Enter book code [D 2 2 4 7 9 8]

3 Fuel your imagination online!

www.av2books.com

AV² Storytime Navigation

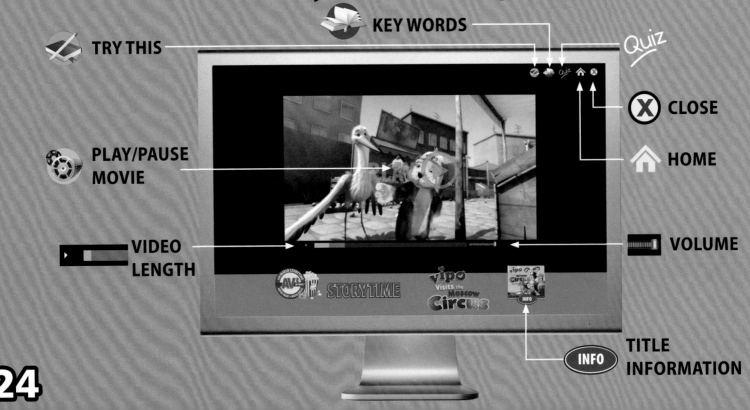

KEY WORDS

Quiz

TRY THIS

X CLOSE

PLAY/PAUSE MOVIE

🏠 HOME

VIDEO LENGTH

VOLUME

STORYTIME · vipo Visits the Moscow Circus · INFO

INFO — TITLE INFORMATION